Skylar's Story:

"Hi! I'm Skylar and I love bearded dragons. My own pet beardie is named Spikes. I got her when I was 7 years old. Spikes loves to eat blueberries and crickets. I take Spikes to lots of places and she always makes people smile. Thank you for buying this coloring book! I like to draw and color too."

Scan QR Code

Facebook: Skylar's Animal Shows
Instagram: Skylar's Animal Shows
YouTube: SkylarsAnimalShows
www.SkylarsAnimalShows.com

This Book
Belongs To:

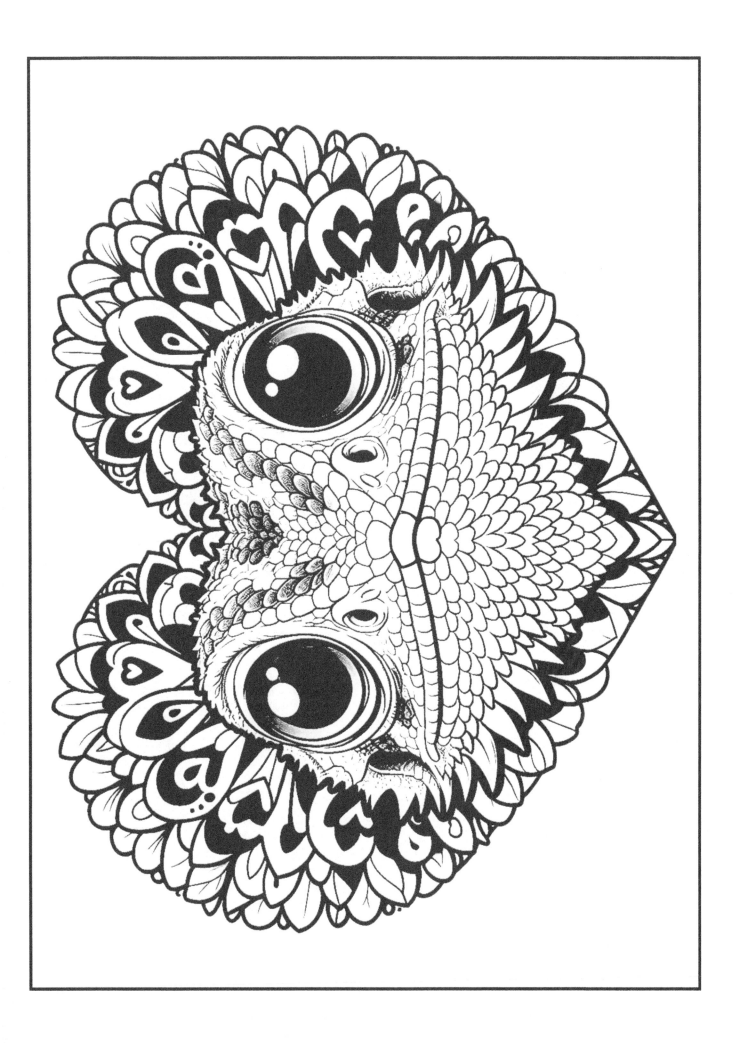

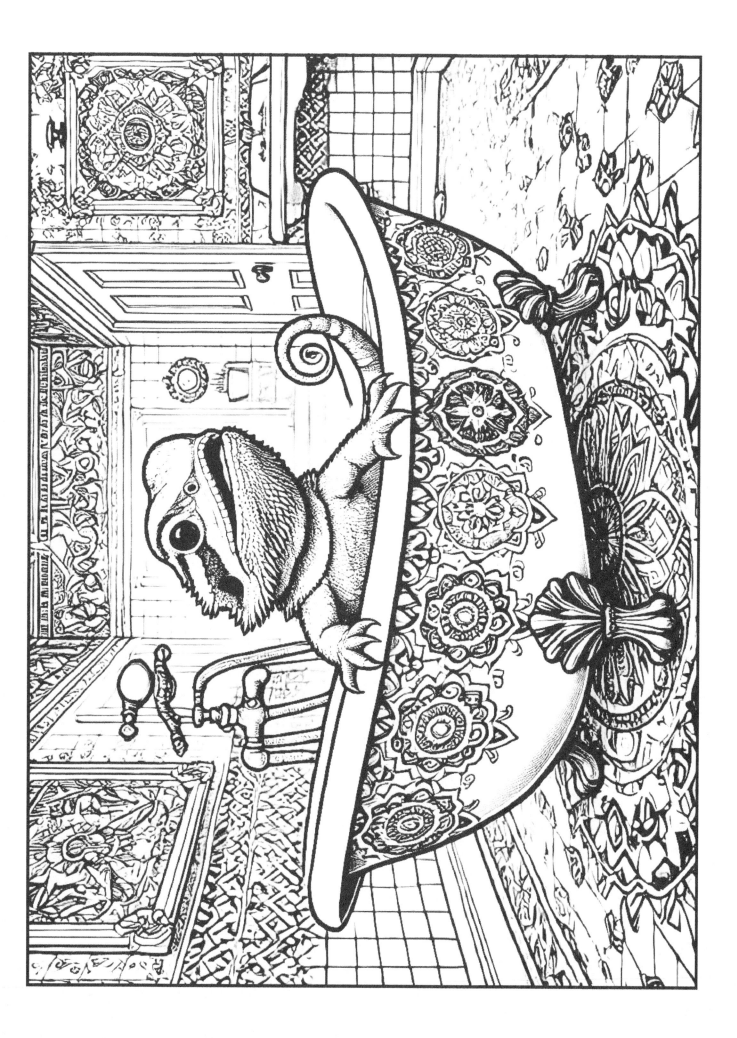

Your feedback is greatly appreciated!

It's through your feedback, support and reviews that Skylar and Spikes are able to create the best books possible and serve more people.

Skylar would be extremely grateful if you could take just 60 seconds to kindly leave an honest review of the book on Amazon. Please share your feedback and thoughts for others to see.

To do so, simply find the book on Amazon's website (or wherever you purchased the book from) and locate the section to leave a review. Select a star rating and write a couple of sentences.

That's it! Thank you so much for your support.

Review this product

Share your thoughts with other customers

Write a customer review

Made in the USA
Coppell, TX
22 September 2024

37493631R00059